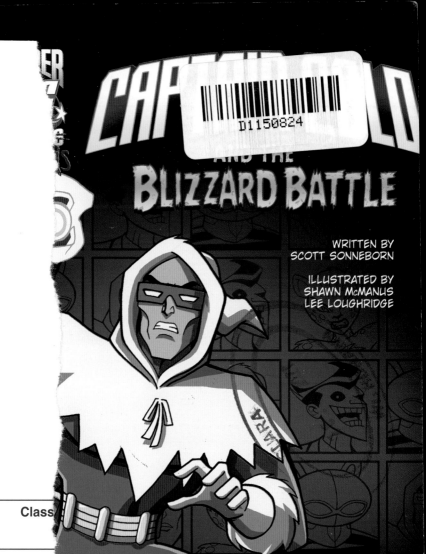

CAPTAIN COLD
AND THE
BLIZZARD BATTLE

WRITTEN BY
SCOTT SONNEBORN

ILLUSTRATED BY
SHAWN McMANUS
LEE LOUGHRIDGE

Raintree is an imprint of Capstone Global Library Limited, a company
incorporated in England and Wales having its registered office at 7 Pilgrim
Street, London, EC4V 6LB – Registered company number: 6695582

To contact Raintree please phone 0845 6044371, fax + 44 (0) 1865 312263,
or email myorders@raintreepublishers.co.uk. Customers from outside the UK
please telephone +44 1865 312262.

First published by Stone Arch Books in 2012
First published in the United Kingdom in 2013
The moral rights of the proprietor have been asserted.

Originated by Capstone Global Library Ltd
Printed and bound in China by Leo Paper Products Ltd

ISBN 978 1 406 26665 8
17 16 15 14 13
10 9 8 7 6 5 4 3 2 1

British Library Cataloguing in Publication Data
A full catalogue record for this book is available from the British Library.

CONTENTS

REAL NAME:
Leonard Snart

OCCUPATION:
Professional Criminal

HEIGHT: 1.88 metres

WEIGHT: 89 kilograms

EYES: Brown

HAIR: Brown

BIOGRAPHY:

Leonard Snart once terrorized Central City with a spree of cold-hearted crimes. No one could escape Captain Cold's icy grip — until the Flash showed up and put the super-villain on ice! Snart knew if he wanted to stay out of jail, he'd have to find a way to combat his super-speedy rival. So, he created an ultra-cold cannon that is capable of bringing even the Scarlet Speedster to a standstill! With the tide turned, Captain Cold looks to use this advantage to

Cold-gun

Snow goggles

Ice grenades

Snow parka

POWERS/ABILITIES:
Wields a cold-gun that can lower
any object's temperature to
absolute zero; his nerves of ice and
his cold heart let him remain cool
and collected even when the heat is
on; he's also a skilled marksman.

CHAPTER 1

SNOW DAY

It was hot. A drop of sweat ran down Myron's forehead. Like all the other kids in Mrs McNabb's Year 5 class, Myron was counting the days until the summer holidays.

"It's still 10 days away!" Myron grumbled to himself. He squirmed in his slimy seat. The window was open, but that didn't help. It was 32 degrees outside – and even hotter in the classroom. Myron couldn't see anything that could save him from another seven sweaty hours in school.

The boy looked out the window and saw that it was starting to snow! At first it was just a few flakes. Then, the flakes became flurries. Soon, the snow was pouring down so heavily that he couldn't see anything at all!

All the kids in the classroom crowded around the window. They couldn't believe what was happening, and neither could the Headmaster. He had no choice but to announce that he was sending everyone home. "This has never happened before in the history of Vinecliff Avenue School," stammered the Headmaster. "But I am forced to call a snow day. . . in July!"

"WOO-HOO!" All the kids cheered!

The loudest shouts came from Myron. He was saved.

*   *   *

"We're doomed!" cried the driver of the armoured van. The snow was more than a metre thick on the street in front of Vinecliff Avenue School. All the cars and vans were stuck, including the armoured van.

"We're completely doomed!" repeated the armoured van's driver. It was all he could think to say. The guard sitting next to him just nodded. His face was frozen in fear. He was looking through the windshield – right at Captain Cold!

Underneath the hood of his parka, Cold smiled wickedly. He had used his cold-gun to lower the temperature of the moisture in the air. The tiny droplets of water had frozen into snow. The villain's blizzard was only big enough to cover the neighbourhood that included Vinecliff Avenue.

However, that area was more than enough. The neighbourhood also held the Central City Central Bank – and the armoured van parked outside it.

Coolly and calmly, Captain Cold raised his cold-gun again.  He froze the armoured van's front doors, trapping the guard and the driver inside. As he walked around to the back, the icy villain dialled his cold-gun down to its coldest setting – absolute zero.

He blasted the solid steel doors on the back of the armoured van. The doors became as cold and brittle as ice.

SMAASSSHHHH!

With a single punch, he shattered the steel doors.

"Now that's cool!" shouted Cold, as he looked at the money inside.

He quickly filled a bag with loot. Then Captain Cold smiled icily. His crime was perfect, and now all he had to do was slip away.

Captain Cold heaved the sack of money over his shoulder. He couldn't have been happier. . . until he saw the Flash running right at him!

CHAPTER 2

TOPPED

ZOOOM! The Flash zoomed towards Captain Cold. The hero's feet moved so quickly that they melted a path straight through the snow.

"Looks like I'm in for a fight!" said Captain Cold. He pulled out his cold-gun, ready for anything. But he wasn't prepared for what happened next.

The Flash ran right past him! Captain Cold couldn't believe it.

The Flash didn't even stop to look at his arch-enemy. He just said, "I'll deal with you later!" And then he raced towards the bank.

Why didn't Flash try to stop me? wondered Captain Cold. *Maybe after all the times we've fought, he's finally learned it's better not to mess with me!*

Suddenly, **BOOM!**

A mountain of ice exploded out through the roof of the bank. On top of it stood a man made entirely of ice. Captain Cold recognized him immediately. The man was the super-villain known as the Icicle. He also used cold powers to commit crimes.

"Nice to see you again, Flash!" shouted the Icicle from the top of the building.

Running at top speed, the Flash raced up the side of the bank.

ZWWWOOOOMMMM!

The Icicle fired a blast that made the wall slick with ice. The Flash slid back down and landed hard on the ground near Captain Cold.

WHAM!

"Captain Cold! What are you doing here?" shouted the Icicle from the bank's rooftop. "Hey, since you *are* here, you should take some notes. You might learn a thing or two from watching the best cold crook in Central City!"

With another blast of ice, the Icicle lifted dozens and dozens of bags of money right out of the bank. "Now this is how you steal some cold hard cash!" boasted the Icicle.

The Flash got back on his feet and rushed up towards the Icicle.

WHOOOOSH!

As the two fought, Captain Cold looked at the single bag he had taken from the armoured van. The Icicle was trying to steal a hundred times as much money. That was why the Flash had run right past Captain Cold and tried to stop the Icicle first.

The Flash and the Icicle were so busy fighting, they didn't even notice Captain Cold slip away. He disappeared into a crowd of people who were all talking about what a dangerous villain the Icicle was.

I robbed the armoured van and got away with the money without having to fight the Flash, thought Captain Cold. *Why am I not happy?*

*   *   *

Inside his hideout, Captain Cold raged. Hours had passed, but he was still upset.

Captain Cold's hideout was a building right in the middle of downtown. The sign on the building said: "Welcome to Central City's only indoor tanning salon and steam sauna!"

A couple of years ago, Captain Cold had used some money he had stolen to buy the place and shut it down. He did that because he hated tanning salons and steam saunas. They were way too hot for his taste. Now, the place made the perfect hideout for a frosty villain like Captain Cold. No one would think to look for him there.

Suddenly, there was a *KNOCK! KNOCK!* at the door. Captain Cold grabbed his cold-gun. Who was it? Had the Flash somehow figured out this was his hideout?

Captain Cold aimed his gun as he slowly opened the door. FWOOOSHHHHHH!!

A man spun into the room. The man was the super-villain known as the Top. He stopped spinning as soon as he saw Captain Cold's cold-gun aimed at him.

"Hey, watch where you point that thing!" cried the Top. "You were the one who invited me here."

"Yeah, well, you should have called to tell me when you were coming," said Captain Cold. "I thought you might be the Flash. I nearly froze you solid!"

"Aw, even you aren't cold enough to freeze a friend," said the Top with a smile.

Captain Cold raised his cold-gun again, squinting down the sights at his villainous ally. "Oh yeah. . . ?" he said.

Then the super-villain grinned and pulled back the trigger. **ZZZRRRRRTT!**

The cold-gun fired a small blast of ice directly at the Top's pointy nose.

"Ah!" screamed the Top, holding his frosty nose in his hand. "What did you do that for?"

"Bad day," said Captain Cold.

"Tell me about it," the Top replied. "I've had so many run-ins with the law today that my head is spinning."

"You're lucky," said Captain Cold. "No one else does what you do. That means you're automatically the best 'spins-around-fast' villain in the world."

"Thanks! But don't sell yourself short," said the Top. "What would we do without a guy like you?"

"You'd call the Icicle," replied Captain Cold. "Or Mr Freeze. Or any of the other villains who have cold powers. Nowadays, it seems like there are dozens of them!"

"The Icicle is the worst," he went on. "I hate that guy. Why does he think he's so great? Wasn't I the one who stole ten thousand dollars this morning?"

"Yup," smiled the Top. "And the Icicle got away with a million!"

"You mean he got away from the Flash?" said the Captain. "With that much money? Okay, I admit, that is a good haul. But wasn't I the one who put Paris's famous Eiffel Tower on ice last year?"

"That was right before the Icicle froze all of Germany!" the Top said. "I hate to say it, but I know when a guy's been topped."

Captain Cold sighed bitterly. The Top was right.

"I'm the man who mastered absolute zero," he said, "but the Icicle is committing better cold crimes than I am. It wouldn't be so bad if he weren't such a show-off."

"He is kind of a jerk," agreed the Top.

"I'd love to put him in his place," growled Captain Cold.

"So why don't you?" asked the Top.

Captain Cold looked at his cold-gun. "I've been sitting here all afternoon, trying to think of a way to do just that. I can create pretty much the same kind of cold as he can," he said. "But I need my gun to do it. Without this weapon, I'm just a regular guy. The Icicle's whole body is made out of solid ice!"

"Think about it," continued Captain Cold. "If I were to hit him with a cold blast, it probably wouldn't hurt him. But one of his icy blasts could certainly hurt me."

The Top shivered and then let out a tremendous sneeze. *ACHOOOOOOOO!* "I guess that means you can't stop him with your cold-gun," he said, sniffling through his frozen nose.

"Maybe not." Captain Cold looked at his gun. Suddenly, his frosty frown broke into a smile. "But I just thought of a way that I can use my gun to beat him!"

CHAPTER 3

UNCOMMON COLD

Standing on top of his downtown hideout, Captain Cold took another sip of orange juice. It had been just over a day since he had figured out how he could beat the Icicle. Since then, he had been working non-stop.

"There's just one more thing I have to do," he said to himself. Captain Cold carefully opened up a small vial. Inside the tiny tube was a specially designed serum. Cold drank it, washing it down with the last drop of orange juice from the carton.

Now I'm ready! he thought. Then he took out his cold-gun and fired it.

The gun lowered the temperature in the air. At its coldest setting, the gun could freeze the air, creating snow or ice over a small area. But Captain Cold had just spent the past day tinkering with the gun, so it could also do something else. Instead of making a small area very cold, it was now making the whole city a little bit icy.

Instead of causing a deep freeze, Captain Cold was dropping all of Central City by seven degrees. On its own, the drop in temperature was enough to cause an outbreak of sore throats and sniffles. But Captain Cold had something far more sinister in mind, which is why he had broken into Bosh Labs earlier that day.

One was an experimental hypothermic rhinovirus. It was in a small package that Captain Cold now took out of his pocket. He opened the package, releasing the virus into the air.

Thanks to the sudden chill in the air Captain Cold had created, everyone in Central City would soon be feeling under the weather. That would weaken their bodies' defences and allow the experimental rhinovirus to spread like wildfire. Soon everyone in Central City would be infected.

Captain Cold wouldn't get sick, thanks to the orange juice and, more importantly, the antidote serum he'd also stolen. But soon, everyone else in Central City would be too weak to stand, including the police and the Flash!

They would be too sick to do anything to stop him. All he had to do was pick which bank he wanted to rob first.

Captain Cold smiled. "Rhinovirus" was the scientific name for the common cold. He was about to conquer the entire city with a super-powerful cold! That had to be the greatest "cold crime" in history.

"Let's see the Icicle top this!" he said with a laugh.

*   *   *

In less than hour, the epidemic spread across Central City. Office workers slumped over their desks, too weak to even sit up. Outside, people were overcome with chills and fever. The guard at the Central City Central Bank felt worse. He coughed and wheezed as Captain Cold strode up to him.

"Stop," moaned the pale and sickly-looking guard.

Captain Cold gave him a small push. The guard toppled to the ground. He was too shaky from his fever to get back up.

"Not feeling well?" asked Captain Cold with a laugh.

The guard's only reply was a hacking cough.

"Well, do you want to say something to the villain who unleashed this diabolical virus on Central City?" asked Captain Cold.

"I will when I see him," wheezed the guard. "I don't know how the Icicle came up with such an evil plan."

"The Icicle?" said Captain Cold. "What do you mean?"

"I know," said the guard, coughing. "This is really low – even for him."

"No, it's not," stammered Captain Cold. "Because he didn't do this. I did!"

"Oh, come on – *ACHOO!*" snuffled the guard. "Everyone knows it was the Icicle. It's all over the news."

The guard pointed a shaky finger at a nearby television. On the screen, a newswoman was saying, "Once again, our top story: The outbreak of this mysterious epidemic has spread quickly thanks to the sudden drop in temperature. Was one of Central City's cold-powered villains responsible? Our reporter caught up with the Icicle and asked him."

Captain Cold's eyes froze to the TV as he watched the Icicle's smirking face.

"You're saying it's because it got colder that everyone's so sick?" said the Icicle. "In that case, Central City's greatest cold villain must be responsible. And that's *me*, of course!" Then, with a smirk, the Icicle froze the reporter.

The newswoman then showed a video of the Chief of Police making a statement at City Hall. "The police and the Flash will catch the villain responsible," promised the ill-looking chief. He had to hold on to the podium to keep from falling over. "We won't stop until the Icicle is behind bars!" he wheezed.

"We just need to get a little rest first," he added weakly.

 Fzzt!

Captain Cold blasted the television.

Captain Cold couldn't believe what he had just seen. His head was spinning.

"Hey, you don't look so good," wheezed the guard. "You look like you're coming down with the Icicle's virus, too."

Captain Cold wasn't sick, but he had never felt so terrible. His worst nightmare was coming true. He had finally committed the best crime of his career. It was a crime that even the Icicle couldn't beat.

And the Icicle was taking all the credit for it!

After all the years he had spent stealing from Central City, Captain Cold finally knew what it felt like to be robbed.

CHAPTER 4

NEW ALLY

Captain Cold was angry. When he got like this, there was only one thing that relaxed him: iced coffee. As he strode into the coffee shop, he was annoyed to see a long line. The people were ordering hot tea to help them feel better. They all wore surgical masks, hoping it would protect them from getting even sicker.

Captain Cold froze everyone in line and walked to the front to place his order.

"One iced coffee," shouted Captain Cold.

Behind the counter, the frightened clerk's hand shook as he gave Captain Cold a cup of steaming hot coffee.

"I said I wanted my coffee iced!" said Captain Cold, even more annoyed. "Never mind, I'll do it myself."

FZZT! FZZT! Captain Cold froze the clerk, and then iced the coffee with his cold-gun. He took a sip. It cheered him up a little.

WHAM! Suddenly, there was a loud noise outside the coffee shop. Captain Cold turned. Through the window, he saw the Flash. He was battling the Icicle through the streets of downtown.

And the Flash was losing! He was too sick to put up much of a fight.

"The Icicle is going to beat the Flash, because of the virus," realized Captain Cold. "A virus the Flash wouldn't have if it weren't for me!"

*   *   *

"ACHOO!" sneezed the Top as he knocked on the door to Captain Cold's hideout. "Have you heard the news?" he coughed. "The Icicle and the Flash are fighting. And the Icicle's about to put the Flash on ice – permanently!"

Captain Cold quickly opened the door to his hideout. "Quick! Get inside," he said. "I wouldn't want anyone to see you out here. A hideout isn't much good if its not a secret!"

The Top sneezed as he spun inside.

"Sorry about the cold," said Cold.

"What are you apologizing for?" snuffled the Top. "The Icicle gave everyone in town this virus. I saw him say so on the news. That's the reason he's the only one not sneezing."

Then the Top gave Captain Cold a curious look.

"Hey, wait!" said the Top. "You're not sneezing either!"

"The only reason the Icicle isn't sneezing is because he is made of solid ice," said Captain Cold, coldly. "He can't catch a cold. I couldn't hurt him with this cold any more than I could with a freeze blast from my cold-gun."

"Wait," cried the Top as he rubbed his nose. "You're saying you gave everyone this – ACHOO – cold?"

"Of course!" shouted Captain Cold. "I am Captain Cold, aren't I?"

"Maybe so," said the Top. "But it looks like the Icicle is about to go down in history as the villain who beat the Flash!"

"Not if I can help it," said Captain Cold.

"What're you going to do?" replied the Top. "They're fighting in the streets right now. Flash won't last much longer. Icicle's going to destroy him!"

"Unless I stop the Icicle," said Captain Cold, coolly.

"That would mean saving your worst enemy – and mine!" said the Top with a sniffle. "If you could, that is. No offence, but you said it yourself. You're just a guy with a cold-gun. The Icicle is made of ice. Your cold blasts can't hurt him, but. . ."

"The Icicle can hurt me," finished Captain Cold.

The Top nodded and then sneezed. "That doesn't sound like a fight you can win."

"Maybe not," agreed Captain Cold, "but I'm going to fight him anyway."

CHAPTER 5

BIG CHILL

The Icicle fired three daggers of ice at the Flash. **CLINK CLANK! CLINK** The daggers of ice hit the ground.

The Flash had been fast enough to dodge them. But the virus he had was making him weaker by the moment. He had to stop to catch his breath.

The Icicle noticed and smiled. **FZzzT!** He fired another dagger at the Flash.

KRAK! The dagger hit a wall of ice created by Captain Cold's cold-gun!

"What are you doing?" cried the Icicle.

Cold didn't answer. Instead he fired an avalanche of ice from his cold-gun. The frozen tidal wave poured over the Icicle. **BOOM!** The Icicle blasted it away.

"Wait, I get it," said the Icicle. "You're the one who really made everyone sick, aren't you? And now you're mad because I took credit for it. OK, I apologize. Now move out of the way and let the better cold villain finish off the Flash!"

"I'm not going to let you do that. Everyone already thinks you committed MY greatest crime," snarled Captain Cold. "There's no way I'm letting you get the credit for finishing the Flash, too."

"You want the Flash," smiled Captain Cold, "you have to go through me."

"You just made a big mistake," snarled the Icicle. "You and I do the same thing. Only I do it better! But if you want a Blizzard Battle – you got it!"

FZZT! He shot an ice dagger straight at Captain Cold.

Captain Cold blocked the dagger with a shield of ice from his cold-gun. **BZZT!** Captain Cold fired back at the Icicle, creating a massive battering ram. **KRAK!** The Icicle cracked it in half with a giant ice spear. Then he raised his hands and hurled a massive blizzard at Captain Cold.

The city froze as the two fought. Glaciers covered streets. A frozen building collapsed under its own weight. As the battle raged, one thing became clear. Captain Cold wasn't hurting the Icicle, but the Icicle was hurting him.

Captain Cold could do only one thing. He ran. **FzziT! FzziT! FzziT!** Ice daggers flew past him as he raced down the street. Captain Cold made it back to his hideout and quickly ducked inside.

ZZRRRRTT! The Icicle tore the building open with a massive blast of ice. He looked around and saw all of Captain Cold's equipment inside.

"So this is your hideout?" smirked the Icicle as he stepped inside. "Now everyone's going to know where it is! A hideout's not much good if it's not secret. It was pretty dumb for you to lead me here!"

"I don't think it was dumb at all!" replied Captain Cold as he threw a lever. The saunas and indoor tanning beds turned on. Suddenly, it was a scorching 40 degrees inside the building.

The Icicle's ice powers would be gone in seconds!

"What do you think you're doing?" cried the Icicle.

"I'm turning up the heat!" shouted Captain Cold. "Now we're going to see which one of us is more cold-blooded."

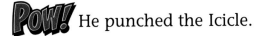 He punched the Icicle.

The Icicle tried to fight back. But without his powers, he didn't know what to do. **WHAM!** Captain Cold hit him again. The Icicle wasn't smirking anymore. He looked scared.

"It takes more than ice powers to make a man cold," said Captain Cold. "I always knew I was colder than you!"

KA-POW! Captain Cold hit the Icicle with an uppercut.

The Icicle stumbled and landed hard on the ground. Captain Cold nudged the fallen villain with his boot. The Icicle didn't move. He was out!

"They say revenge is a dish best served cold," said the Captain, wiping sweat from his eyes. "But it also tastes pretty good hot!"

But before he had time to enjoy his victory — **ZOOOM!** The Flash raced in. He was still sick, but Captain Cold had given him time to catch his breath.

BZZZT! Captain Cold tried to pull the trigger on his cold-gun, but the Flash was too fast.

SNAP! The Flash yanked away Captain Cold's gun.

WHAM! He knocked Captain Cold to the ground with a single punch.

"I just don't understand super-villains," said the Flash. "It was so easy to follow the icy path of destruction that led here. So now I know where your hideout is, which means it isn't good for anything anymore. And with the Icicle out cold and your gun out of your hands, I won't have any problem taking both of you to jail."

"Was all of that really worth it?" asked the Flash. "Just so everyone would know you were the one who unleashed this sickness on the city?"

Captain Cold didn't say anything. He was too busy smiling. The Flash knew who had created the virus! Soon, everyone else would know that the villain responsible for the greatest cold crime ever committed in Central City was him – Captain Cold!

BIOGRAPHIES

Scott Sonneborn has written dozens of books, one circus (for Ringling Bros. Barnum & Bailey), and a bunch of TV shows. He's been nominated for one Emmy and spent three very cool years working at DC Comics. He lives in Los Angeles, USA with his wife and their two sons.

Shawn McManus has been drawing pictures ever since he was able to hold a pencil in his tiny little hand. Since then, he has illustrated comic books including Sandman, Batman, Dr. Fate, Spider-Man, and many others. Shawn has also done work for film, animation, and online entertainment. He lives in New England, USA, and he loves the spring season there.

Lee Loughridge has been working in comics for more than 18 years. He currently lives in sunny California, USA in a tent on the beach.

GLOSSARY

absolute zero lowest possible temperature. At 273.15 degrees celsius below zero, the particles that make up all matter would stop moving.

diabolical extremely wicked or evil

doomed fated to suffer terribly

experimental new or not tested thoroughly

outbreak sudden start of something such as disease or war

serum a liquid used to prevent or cure a disease

shatter break into tiny pieces

unleash set loose or abandon control of something

uppercut punch or other kind of attack that is directed upward towards the target's chin

DISCUSSION QUESTIONS

1. The Flash is super-fast. Captain Cold uses his cold-gun to freeze whatever he pleases. Which power would you rather have? Why?

2. The Icicle's weakness is heat. Do you have any weaknesses? What are your strengths? Discuss your answers.

3. This book has 10 illustrations. Which one is your favourite? Why?

WRITING PROMPTS

1. Captain Cold thinks the Icicle is copying him. Has anyone ever copied something you did? What happened? Write about your copycat experience.

2. The Icicle is heated up by Captain Cold. What are some other ways Captain Cold could have stopped the Icicle? Write about it.

3. Captain Cold made his secret hideout in a former tanning salon. If you could have a secret base anywhere in the world, where would you put it? Write about your secret base, then draw a picture of it.